Helping families of all species, one tadpole at a time.

Freeda the Frog™

Says Farewell to Her Fish

by Gold Mom's Choice Award® winner
Nadine Haruni

art by Tina Modugno

Foreword

When I first came upon Freeda the Frog, I instantly connected with the goal and mission of this series. Freeda the Frog is an exceptionally well-written set of books that teaches kids acceptance of various family issues, which can be both difficult and tumultuous for children. Additionally, this series fosters their overall awareness and ability to cope during these challenges.

Nadine Haruni has done a wonderful job creating child-friendly language that conveys and builds an understanding of issues such as divorce, moving to a new school/town, and even the topic of various family structures such as step-families, mixed race, religion, and ethnicity. This fourth book in the series, *Freeda the Frog Says Farewell to Her Fish* explores yet another very important topic many children experience: loss, specifically the loss of a pet.

I can attest to this series' effectiveness in helping children navigate and cope with the challenges and hardships of turbulent life events.

– Huma Imtiaz, school psychologist in New York

www.mascotbooks.com

Freeda the Frog™ Says Farewell to Her Fish

©2019 Nadine Haruni. All Rights Reserved. No part of this publication may be reproduced, stored in a retrieval system or transmitted in any form by any means electronic, mechanical, or photocopying, recording or otherwise without the permission of the author.

For more information, please contact:
Mascot Books
620 Herndon Parkway #320
Herndon, VA 20170
info@mascotbooks.com

Library of Congress Control Number: 2018913167

CPSIA Code: PRT0219A
ISBN: 978-1-64307-285-2

Printed in the United States

This book is dedicated to my mom, husband Jon, and the special tadpoles in my life: Jake, Sam, Hannah, Adi, Yael, Max, Kayla, and Emma—whose love and support helped make this happen. I would also like to thank my brother Eric, who helped provide inspiration for parts of this story.

I would also like to dedicate this book to all of the courageous little tadpoles who have suffered the loss of a pet or other loved one. Try to cherish the memories with them and remember...
"It is better to have loved and lost, than never to have loved at all."
– Alfred Lord Tennyson

Freeda, Samson, and their tadpoles were loving life at their new family lily pad in the lovely town of Port Frogafly. Moving from their old home in Frogelot was a little difficult at first, but everyone was really happy in Port Frogafly.

One day, Frannie came home from school with a flyer about the big Port Frogafly County Fair. It was that night.
"Can we go?" Frannie asked.
"Please? Please?" chimed in Frank and Jack. "All of our new friends will be there."
"That does sound like fun," Freeda said to Samson.
"It does!" said Samson. "Let's go!"
"Ribbit! Ribbit!" the tadpoles yelled out. (That was frog-talk for "Woo-hoo!")

When they got to the fair, Frannie, Frank, and Jack saw their tadpole buddies from school, Kyle, Emerson, and Maxine. Together, the group spent the day exploring the fair's crazy rides, great games, and tasty food. It was so much fun!

As the day came to an end, Jack wanted to play one last game. "Can I please play?" he asked. "I want to win a pet goldfish!"

Freeda and Samson weren't necessarily sure they were ready for a pet, but they let Jack play anyway.

Jack was a natural! Everyone watched as Jack threw the darts and popped one, then two, then three balloons!

"Ribbit! Ribbit!" Jack shouted.
"We have a new pet!" yelled Frannie. "What should we call her?
Mrs. Swiggles? Fido? What about Princess?"
"How about Goldie?" suggested Jack.
"She looks like a Goldie," said Frannie, smiling.
"Welcome to the family, Goldie!" said Samson.

6

The family took Goldie home and put her in a fish tank that Frannie, Frank, and Jack had picked out. They made it extra cozy, and Goldie seemed to really enjoy her new home.

The tadpoles all loved having a pet. Every day after school they'd come home and take turns feeding and playing with Goldie. As the months passed, Goldie became a cherished member of the family.

One day after school, Frannie, Frank, and Jack came home with Kyle, Emerson, and Maxine for a playdate. Of course, the first thing they did was go to feed Goldie. But something wasn't right.

Goldie was moving slower than usual, she was shivering, and her lips were turning blue. They immediately called their parents to let them know. Freeda and Samson then called the pet doctor, who told them to bring Goldie in right away.

The tadpoles anxiously waited for Freeda and Samson to return from the doctor's office. But when Freeda and Samson came home several hours later, they didn't have Goldie with them.

"She's very sick," Freeda explained. "They're keeping her overnight to see if they can help her feel better."

"How long will she be there?" Jack asked.

"They're not sure," said Samson, "but we can go visit her tomorrow to cheer her up."

The next day, everyone went to the hospital to visit Goldie. The tadpoles brought her toy seahorse and her favorite chocolate-covered seaweed to try to cheer her up. When Goldie saw her family, she managed to give them a small smile, but she was very weak and tired.

Before long, the doctor came in and told them that she was too sick for visitors, and that it would be best if they went home and let her get some rest.

The phone rang early the next morning. No one had slept very well. Freeda picked up the phone and the family gathered around. It was the doctor.

When Freeda hung up the phone, she cried. "The doctor said they did everything they could, but Goldie didn't make it through the night."

Samson pulled Freeda and the tadpoles in for a tight hug.

That night at dinner, everyone was quiet. Freeda and Samson tried to smile as they ate their favorite dinner of flies, but it was tough for them, too.

"Losing Goldie is extremely difficult," said Freeda. "She really became a beloved part of our family."

"This is a hard time for all of us," added Samson. "Just know that you can talk to us, your grandparents, your friends, or your favorite teachers at school whenever you are sad. It helps to let your feelings out, and I'm sure other friends who have also lost a pet will know exactly what you're going through."

The next day at school, the tadpoles told Kyle, Emerson, and Maxine the sad news.

"It's really hard to lose someone you love," said Kyle. "We still miss our starfish who died last year, but it gets easier over time."

"When our pet jellyfish died, we all got together and shared our favorite memories before we said goodbye," said Emerson.

"That's a good idea," said Maxine. "Be sure to remember all the good times you had with Goldie."

When the tadpoles came home from school, they told Freeda about the conversation with their friends.

"We'd like to have a ceremony so we can say goodbye to Goldie," suggested Jack.
"What a great idea," said Freeda.

The next day, Freeda, Samson, and the tadpoles went into the backyard and buried Goldie next to her favorite spot—near the small tree on their pad. They each said a few words about Goldie, remembering the great times they had together and the special relationship each one of them had with her.

Jack was the last one to speak. "Goldie really helped make our new house feel even more like a home, and we were very lucky to have her."

Goldie
Beloved Pet
and Friend

The family then
joined together for a big
family hug as they said a final
goodbye to their friend Goldie.

Discussion Questions

1. Have you ever had a pet?

2. If the pet is no longer alive, were there things you did to make it easier for you to deal with the loss?

3. Do you agree that pets become part of the family?

4. Did you ever lose something or someone else who was important to you?

5. Did you talk to a friend, family member, or teacher about it, and did that help?

6. Do you think it's important to talk about your feelings with someone instead of just keeping them inside?

7. What is the best thing about having a pet?

8. If you've never had a pet, why would you want one and what kind of pet would you want?

9. Do you think pets can show you that they love you? If so, give some examples where you have seen a pet react to you or someone you know that showed how they felt.

For additional information about the *Freeda the Frog*™ Children's Book series, Freeda the Frog™ products, Freeda the Frog™ news and events, and to order additional copies of any of the Freeda the Frog™ books, go to www.freedathefrog.com. Also be sure to follow Freeda the Frog™ on Instagram, Twitter, and Facebook @freedathefrog!

Check out the other books in the Freeda The Frog™ Children's Book series!

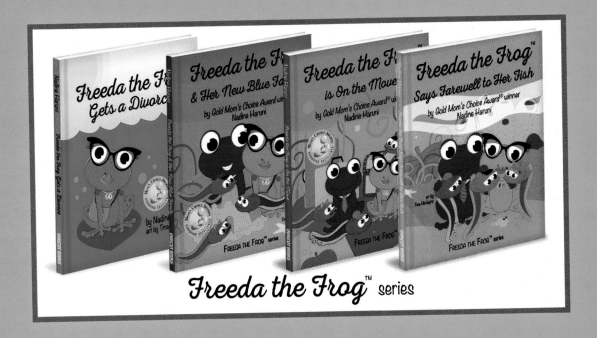

Freeda the Frog™ series

Draw a picture of your favorite pet or animal!

Take Freeda with you on your family adventures! Color and cut out this Freeda pic, glue a popsicle stick to the back of it and *voila*—Flat Freeda! Then tag us in your pics at @Freedathefrog and message them to us on Facebook or Instagram for us to re-post.

Cut along the dotted lines for your very own bookmark!

Freeda the Frog™
Says Farewell to Her Fish

by Nadine Haruni   art by Tina Modugno

About the Author

Nadine Haruni is the author of the Gold Mom's Choice Award® winning *Freeda the Frog*™ Children's Book series, which focuses on different family situations and helping children cope with various life issues. Nadine is a member of the Society of Children's Book Writers and Illustrators and the Independent Book Publishers Association. Aside from writing, she teaches yoga and is a practicing attorney. Nadine is married with five children.

The first book of the series, *Freeda the Frog Gets a Divorce*, focuses on the difficult circumstances for children surrounding their parents' divorce. The second book, *Freeda the Frog & Her New Blue Family*, focuses on blended/step-families, as well as families of mixed race, religion, or ethnicity. The third book of the series, *Freeda the Frog is On the Move*, is geared toward helping kids cope with a move to a new school and/or new town. This fourth book focuses on dealing with the loss of a pet. Stay tuned for Nadine's future *Freeda the Frog*™ books, where Freeda and the tadpoles continue to help kids face more of life's challenges.